UNCLE GRANDPA

My Left or Yours?

HOLD ON TO YOUR PLANET!

by Lloyd Cordill   illustrated by Derek Charm

An Imprint of Penguin Random House

CARTOON NETWORK™ BOOKS

CARTOON NETWORK BOOKS
Penguin Young Readers Group
An Imprint of Penguin Random House LLC

ISBN 978-0-8431-8287-3   10 9 8 7 6 5 4 3 2 1

Good morning!

You are about to embark on a fantastic journey with everyone's favorite uncle and grandpa, Uncle Grandpa! There will be spaceships and danger and maybe a talking ooze—and you get to decide what happens!

Everyone knows that books have pages and words, and taste nothing like grilled cheese sandwiches. But this book is super-different from most books. At the end of every chapter, you will have to help Uncle Grandpa and his friends make a decision. Sometimes you'll have to solve puzzles to figure out what to do next.

During your adventure, you'll collect **BURRITO BADGES**. Burrito Badges are proof of how much you helped Uncle Grandpa. Keep track of the badges you gather, and add them all up at the end of your story to determine your **Burrito Score!**

Good luck!

Inside the front seat of Uncle Grandpa's RV, Uncle Grandpa is gripping the steering wheel with fourteen hands. Normally, Uncle Grandpa has two arms like everyone else, but Uncle Grandpa is rarely normal.

He leans hard on the gas pedal with his foot, and the RV accelerates through a barn, a beauty parlor, a trampoline factory, and Dave's house. Giant Realistic Flying Tiger zooms through the RV-shaped holes in each building, chasing after everyone's favorite Uncle and Grandpa. The race around the world is on!

It all started because Uncle Grandpa ate every burger in the jar of burgers, except one. Pizza Steve wanted the last burger. Mr. Gus wanted the last burger. Uncle Grandpa wanted the last burger, and so did the Uncle Grandpa head sticking out of his armpit. Giant Realistic Flying Tiger roared loudly, which the others knew meant she also wanted the last burger. A race around the world was the only way to decide who would get to eat the last burger in the jar.

Uncle Grandpa takes an early lead, driving around the world in the RV—Uncle Grandpa's totally awesome ride, which is as big as a mansion on the inside, and chock-full of robots and weird foods and secret doors. Giant Realistic Flying Tiger is rainbow flying; Pizza Steve, the coolest piece of pizza in the world, is racing in his totally rad jetboard-

3

glider, which is part jetpack, part skateboard, and *all* hang glider. Jetboard-glider is about the coolest way in the world to race around the world, and so of course *Pizza Steve* is riding one!

Mr. Gus is just walking. Slowly, he puts one green dinosaur foot in front of the other. Obviously, he is in last place.

Uncle Grandpa checks the RV's rearview mirror. Giant Realistic Flying Tiger and Pizza Steve are gaining on him!

"Hey, Belly Bag!" Uncle Grandpa nudges his magical talking fanny pack. "I have a great idea. We should switch the RV into superspeed mode."

"Uncle Grandpa!" Belly Bag licks his zipper in distress. "That's not a great idea. That's a really terrible idea. Don't you remember what happened last time?"

"Gee, let me think." Uncle Grandpa scratches his mustache in thought. "Uhhhhhhhhhmmmmmmmmmmm . . ."

Belly Bag listens nervously.

"NOPE! I don't remember." Uncle Grandpa grabs the lever that says SUPERSPEED MODE and throws it on.

Twenty monster-truck wheels pop out of the bottom of the RV, and forty-twelve jet engines sprout out the back. The engines shoot blue flames, sending the RV rocketing across the Earth, tearing up city streets and blowing over buildings. The RV scares fish silly as it zooms over the oceans.

"Wow!" Uncle Grandpa says in awe.

"WAAAAARGH!" Belly Bag screams.

Not to be outdone, Pizza Steve and Giant Realistic Flying Tiger also pick up speed. They zip around the Earth, faster and faster, until the Earth starts spinning wildly out of control. The Earth spins so fast that it jumps out of its orbit, spiraling like a top, on a collision course with the sun.

"Oh no," Mr. Gus moans, watching the sun grow large and hot in the sky. "You really did it this time, Uncle Grandpa."

The RV skids to a stop in front of the talking dinosaur. Giant Realistic Flying Tiger crashes into the back of the RV at full speed. Pizza Steve crashes into the back of Giant Realistic Flying Tiger. Uncle Grandpa sticks his head out the window of the RV. "Did what, Mr. Gus?"

"The Earth is spinning toward the sun! It's going to crash. Our whole planet is going to be consumed in a ball of fiery gas."

Uncle Grandpa shrugs. "So? That happens to me every time Giant Realistic Flying Tiger eats a burrito."

The lady tiger roars in irritation.

"Besides," Uncle Grandpa adds. "Deep-fried Earth tastes great!"

Mr. Gus says, "Yeah, but we won't be around to taste it if we get cooked!"

"Hmm, good point." Uncle Grandpa nods. "Okay! Time to save the Earth!" The whole gang piles into the RV and Uncle Grandpa starts up the engine. But he forgets that the

RV is still in superspeed mode. The RV rockets into the sky and flies into outer space. The Earth spins away on its collision course with the sun.

"Oh no!" Uncle Grandpa cries. "Earth is escaping!"

The RV crashes into a space station, putting a huge dent in the side so that it starts leaking precious oxygen. (You can't breathe in space without oxygen.)

Inside the space station are a bunch of kid astronauts. They start running around like crazy, putting on their helmets and waving their arms.

Meanwhile, Pizza Steve pops his knuckles and puts his feet up on the dashboard of the RV. "Hey, it's no problem Earth's gonna go barbecue. I'm the coolest guy on the planet Mars! You know, the Red Planet? Our next-door neighbor? The one that looks like *this*?" He points at one of his circles of pepperoni. "I'm even cooler on Mars than I am on Earth. And on Earth, I'm *superfamous.*"

Belly Bag chimes in. "Maybe the Martians will help us save the Earth!"

Mr. Gus says, "Come on, Uncle Grandpa, what should we do?"

If you think Uncle Grandpa should rescue the kids on the Astro School space station, *go to Page 95*.

If you think Uncle Grandpa should ask the Martians for help, *go to Page 37*.

If you think Uncle Grandpa should chase after Earth, *go to Page 40*.

Uncle Grandpa and his friends arrive

to great fanfare at the Martian royal palace. Aliens line up along the main boulevard leading to the crystal castle, throwing red confetti and cheering.

"Wow!" Mr. Gus says, uncustomarily amazed. "They're really happy to see us."

Giant Realistic Flying Tiger roars in agreement.

The Martian warriors take the gang into the castle and straight to the throne room. There, the Martian princess waits for them on her seat carved out of pure ruby.

Never in his whole life has Pizza Steve seen anything as cool as the Martian princess. She wears resplendent crimson robes, has flawless skin and billowing red hair, and she has the legs of an armadillo, which is supercool.

She rises from the throne as the gang approaches. Her voice is like that of a graceful bird. "Greetings, travelers from Earth. At last you have come. I am so thrilled to have finally found you, the chosen one, the one who will bring balance to my kingdom."

Pizza Steve slides across the throne room on his knees, stopping at the princess's feet. He kisses her hand smoothly. "Thank you for the kind words, Princess."

The princess pulls her hand away from his kisses.

"No, silly pizza man. Not you. I mean this one—the chosen one—the hero of Mars!"

Mr. Gus stares at her blankly for a moment. He looks over his shoulder to see if anyone is standing behind him. "Wait, you mean me?"

"Of course, Magnificent Mr. Gus. You are the chosen one!"

"I'm not the chosen one of anything, not even a kickball team."

The princess offers him a sweet smile. "You don't understand. Mars needs a new king. As the princess, I get to choose who it is. And I choose you, Mr. Gus. I choose you!"

"GrrrrrrrRROWL!" Giant Realistic Flying Tiger becomes Giant Realistic Snarling Tiger. It's unclear why she is so upset, but she rainbows out of the throne room in a huff.

Ignoring the interruption, the Martian princess places a gentle hand on Mr. Gus's shoulder. "Come with me, my future king. We must go to the kitchens. You have much to approve before your coronation."

Mr. Gus blushes so hard, the scales on his cheeks turn from green to red. Pizza Steve follows him and the princess into the kitchen. "Wait for me! I will make an excellent king."

Once they're gone, Uncle Grandpa looks around. He's the only person left in the throne room. It's quiet. He's bored and lonely. And he doesn't know what to do.

If Uncle Grandpa checks on Giant Realistic Flying Tiger,

go to Page 111.

If Uncle Grandpa helps the others prep for the coronation,

go to Page 80.

"Cleaning mission complete!" Tiny Miracle sounds proud of his excellent job sorting all the junk in the science lab.

From where his head is resting on a shelf, Uncle Grandpa says, "Great job, Tiny Miracle! . . . Oh. Uh-oh."

It looks like Tiny Miracle got a little carried away while cleaning the lab. Not only did he sort and put away the lab equipment, he sorted and put away Uncle Grandpa, too! His arms and legs are tucked in drawers. His torso is hanging in the closet, and his head, sitting on the shelf, doesn't appear to mind at all.

"Now come on!" Uncle Grandpa says. "Let's save the Earth!"

Mr. Gus frowns. "But Uncle Grandpa! When you're like this, you can't get around. And you can't help."

Ted and Betsy shiver, even though it's burning hot. "But we only have a few minutes before the Earth crashes into the sun."

"Yeah," Uncle Grandpa says. "To put me back together in that time, we're gonna need a tiny miracle."

"Did somebody say Tiny Miracle?"

THE END

Uncle Grandpa grabs his wormhole and shakes it out until it's big enough to fit Earth inside. The whole planet flies through the portal and vanishes.

On the other end, the Earth goes hurtling past the far reaches of space.

"*Whee!*" cheers Uncle Grandpa.

Earth flies so far and so fast that it exits the known universe.

"Whoa!" Pizza Steve marvels at the cosmic light show all around the planet. "Where are we?"

"I wonder what the universe looks like from the outside," Mr. Gus says.

Uncle Grandpa takes them to an empty field on a dark night. "Check it out!" he says, pointing up at the sky.

The gang looks back the way Earth came from. An enormous red bag fills the sky. Its zipper smiles.

The whole universe is tucked inside Belly Bag's mouth. Who would have thought?

"I would!" says Uncle Grandpa.

Wait, you can hear me?

"Good morning!"

THE END

12

Between two of the trees in the dark forest, Mr. Gus sees Uncle Grandpa waving him closer.

"*Scree!*" shrieks the owl. "Uncle Grandpa? Oh no!"

Mr. Gus runs faster and notices that Uncle Grandpa is standing next to an old wooden outhouse. He opens the door. Mr. Gus dives inside, falling through the seat. Uncle Grandpa jumps in after him.

The two friends tumble through empty space. The outhouse was a portal back to the Challenge Room! They vanish from the forest seconds before the giant gray owl crashes into the outhouse.

COLLECT 10 BURRITO BADGES

Go to Page 24.

"Yeah, I think these pieces of wall do go together!"

Uncle Grandpa gives the hood of the RV a swift kick, knocking it out into space. A dozen Uncle Grandpa hands grab all the pieces of space station wall and throw them into place. The scraps of metal fit together like puzzle pieces. The wall is reformed, but the cracks between the pieces are still leaking air.

Belly Bag unzips. Uncle Grandpa reaches inside and pulls out a huge wad of bubblegum. He stuffs his mouth full of the pink stuff and starts chewing, smacking his lips. He chews and chews until his cheeks are swollen. He grabs more gum out of Belly Bag and piles that stuff into his mouth, too.

The others watch in amazement as Uncle Grandpa begins to blow the most epic bubble in the history of bubblegum chewing. It inflates like a smelly pink balloon, growing larger and larger until it fills the whole hallway, pushing the children back.

And then the bulbous ball of bubblegum pops. The sound echoes through the whole station. KA-BOOM! When the others open their eyes, they see Uncle Grandpa standing in the middle of the hall, covered in a pink shroud of soggy bubblegum. The gum has also spattered the walls and ceiling and floors and the round glass helmets the Astro School students are wearing.

"Ta-da!" Uncle Grandpa sings. He points at the broken wall. The gum has filled all the cracks, sealing it tight.

"Pretty cool, Uncle G!" Pizza Steve gives Uncle Grandpa a big thumbs-up. "You really gummed up the works."

Mr. Gus covers his face in embarrassment at Pizza Steve's terrible pun.

"Okay!" Uncle Grandpa says. "One fixed wall. One problem solved. Now we can play games!"

"But, Uncle Grandpa!" Sally moans. "We can't play games. We have to save the Earth. It's going to crash into the sun."

"Oh yeah. For a minute there I forgot. Hmm . . ." Uncle Grandpa thinks carefully, and then says, "Yeah, I still think we should play games."

If you think the Astro School students should try to save Earth, *go to Page 100*.

If you think the Astro School students should play games with Uncle Grandpa, *go to Page 84*.

"Look! The burrito is turning!"

The kids cheer as the flying burrito swerves off course, narrowly missing the giant Uncle Grandpa's mouth.

"Yay!" Mr. Gus pumps his fist in the air.

Pizza Steve removes his shades, blinking in disbelief. "Whoa."

"GrrrrrrrRROWL!" Giant Realistic Flying Tiger roars exuberantly.

Uncle Grandpa applauds. "You did it! Great job, kids. You've stopped the Earth from crashing into the sun."

"No, that's what we *should* be doing," Sally says, sticking her hands on her hips. "But you have us here playing video games instead of helping."

"Wrong!" Uncle Grandpa pulls out the remote that controls the Challenge Room. With a push of a button, all the holograms and virtual reality disappear, revealing a big glass window peering out of the Astro School space station.

Everyone gasps when they see outside. Sure enough, the RV has used its superspeed jet engines to push the Earth clear of the sun, and now it is starting to curve into a new orbit.

"But how?" Sally asks, utterly baffled.

"Simple!" Uncle Grandpa explains. "I created this virtual-reality game. I was looking for inspiration and thought *Hmm . . . the Earth crashing into the sun seems like some pretty good inspiration.* So I made a big burrito be Earth because they both taste great deep-fried, and I made the sun a giant mouth because, you know, the sun and me go way back and we both gobble things up."

The kids all laugh as Uncle Grandpa grins widely, showing off his bright white teeth.

"I told the RV to do to the Earth whatever you kids did to the burrito. And here we are!"

"Wow, Uncle Grandpa," Mr. Gus says. "Now it all makes perfect sense."

Uncle Grandpa wiggles a finger in his ear so far the tip of his finger pokes out of his other ear. "When did it not make sense?"

"Oh, Uncle Grandpa! Ha-ha-ha!" The kids and the others laugh merrily.

"Never change, Uncle G!" Pizza Steve says slyly.

"You got it, buddy." Uncle Grandpa winks. "Now who wants burritos?"

COLLECT 45 BURRITO BADGES

THE END

Trumpets sound a happy fanfare as Mr. Gus climbs the dais and stands before the Martian throne. The coronation is underway.

The Martian princess has dressed Mr. Gus in royal robes, giving him a regal style he has never felt before. The princess smiles and claps at everything. Pizza Steve sits in the front row and cries like he's at a wedding, but really he's crying because he wanted to be the Martian king.

Uncle Grandpa sits in the back beside Giant Realistic Flying Tiger, who still looks dreadfully grumpy. She growls quietly, curling her upper lip.

A wrinkly old priest approaches the throne. He hands an enormous ceremonial battle-ax to the Martian princess. Her skinny arms quiver as she struggles to lift it. She raises the ax above her head and says, "Mr. Gus, to become our liege, all you must do is say these words, and then take this royal ax from my hands: 'I, Mr. Gus, promise to uphold the virtues of the planet Mars. I will be strong. I will be brave. And I will lead us to a better future.'"

Mr. Gus opens his mouth. He is about to speak. This is Uncle Grandpa's moment. If he is going to stop the coronation, it has to be now.

If Uncle Grandpa tries to stop the coronation,
go to Page 88.

If Uncle Grandpa lets the coronation happen,
go to Page 43.

Despite the Astro School students' best attempts, the beautiful burrito—overflowing with cheese and guacamole—plummets into Uncle Grandpa's mouth. CRUNCH!

"Oh no!" says the giant Uncle Grandpa. "I think I'm gonna—ah . . . ah . . . ah . . . ACHOO!"

The giant Uncle Grandpa lets out a tremendous sneeze, and hundreds of burritos shoot out of his nostrils. The burritos rain down on the floor of the Challenge Room.

"YAY! BURRITOS!" the kids cheer. They devour the tasty food hungrily.

Everything seems to be back to normal. The virtual reality generators of the Challenge Room create a tranquil sunny field covered in green grass. The kids and teachers sit beneath a big oak tree and enjoy their burrito lunch. Mr. Gus, Pizza Steve, Giant Realistic Flying Tiger, and of course Uncle

20

Grandpa share the feast.

"This is really nice!" Sally says around a mouthful of burrito.

"Yeah," Uncle Grandpa says, stretching out on his back and looking up at the artificially generated sky. "But I feel like we're forgetting something."

"Yeah." Mr. Gus scratches his head. "I feel that way, too."

"Oh well!" Uncle Grandpa yawns loudly.

And then Earth crashes into the sun. KA-BOOM!

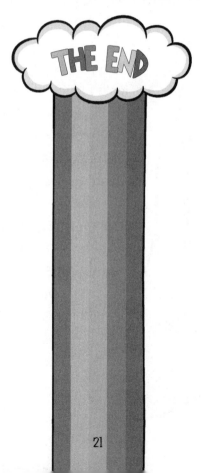

THE END

"I have the code!" Uncle Grandpa says, his chin transforming into a bugle, which he toots to declare his triumph. "Start the calculation machine!"

The calculation machine is a massive metal box in the center of the laboratory. It has sharp corners and spinning gears and rollers that eat and spit out bits of magnetic tape.

Huddled in a corner of the lab are Beary Nice and Hot Dog Person.

"Hey, Hot Dog Person! It looks like we need to help save the Earth." Beary Nice sounds chipper, as always.

"Yeah," Hot Dog Person drones sullenly. "I guess you're right."

"Hmm . . ." Beary Nice picks up some of the spilled tape and examines it. "These calculations are beary nice. Hey! That's me!"

Hot Dog Person inches over to the machine, where the gears are spinning quickly. "Hmm . . . hey, Beary, I think I've figured out how to calculate the—"

Hot Dog Person's bun gets caught on one of the gears and he's yanked inside the calculation machine, where he's ground up into a hamburger person.

"Oh no!" Beary Nice covers his furry cheeks with his paws. "Hot Dog Person broke the machine. Now we'll never complete our calculations."

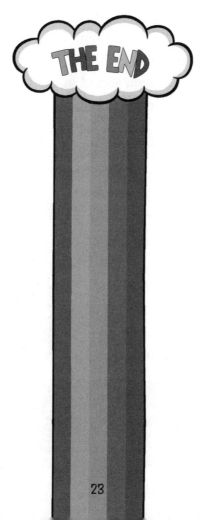

After falling through empty space for several minutes, Mr. Gus and Uncle Grandpa land safely in the Challenge Room. The students of Astro School are trying to guide an enormous holographic burrito through the air. But the burrito is headed straight toward an even enormous-er Uncle Grandpa mouth.

Sally flies around the burrito, barking orders. "More to the right! Don't let Uncle Grandpa eat our giant burrito."

The kids struggle to push the burrito off course. Mr. Gus rushes forward to help. Uncle Grandpa watches the scene, smiling and nodding with satisfaction.

Figure out a way to keep the giant Uncle Grandpa mouth from eating the burrito.

If you fail, *go to Page 20*.

If you succeed, *go to Page 16*.

Huge green muscles bulge out of Mr. Gus's arms. With a tremendous display of strength he grabs the falling stones and jams them back into place.

"RAH! Take that, loose ceiling tiles!" He growls and lashes out his tail to catch the last falling stone. It balances impressively on the tip of his tail.

"Nice going, Mr. Gus!" The dinosaur man looks up and sees that one of the ceiling stones has transformed into a squashed statue of Uncle Grandpa. Mr. Gus lets go and Uncle Grandpa drops back to the floor, morphing into his original shape.

The gang continues through the cave. They follow a narrow tunnel for several miles, and are so tired from walking they are about to give up and turn back, when they hear voices in the distance.

"Yet can home go we?"

"No. Down way sure I'm I heard this voices."

Belly Bag quakes in his waistband. "Who could it be, Uncle Grandpa?"

Uncle Grandpa mumbles, "Gee, I don't know."

"Quiet!" Mr. Gus whispers. "They're going to hear us."

ZIIIIIIP! Belly Bag zips his mouth shut.

An immense shadow stretches across the sides of the tunnel as the voices get louder.

"Hear you that did? Teeth metal like sounded together clasp pulled a by being it."

"Observations your Globble astute always as are."

Suddenly, two ooze aliens appear before Uncle Grandpa and the others. They're the size of grizzly bears, bright green, and a little bit see-through.

"Egads! It's a pair of Glops!" Uncle Grandpa cowers behind Pizza Steve.

One of the ooze aliens hides behind the other, but remembers they're both see-through so it doesn't really matter. The lead alien squeals, "Eek! Aliens of a pack!"

"Uhhh . . . take us to your leader?" Uncle Grandpa doesn't know what else to say.

"Them grab!" The ooze aliens charge toward the gang, and then everything goes black.

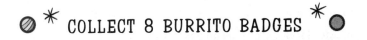

COLLECT 8 BURRITO BADGES

Go to Page 113.

"Okay, Sally, teacher lady, other kids, hop in the RV! We're going for a ride!" Uncle Grandpa bangs on the hood and the RV opens up. The group rushes inside.

As they hurry aboard, the space station starts to rumble.

"Uh-oh!" Pizza Steve says nervously. "This does not look cool at all."

When the last of the kids is aboard the RV, Uncle Grandpa hops behind the steering wheel and backs out of the space station. In the living room, the kids and their teachers are settling into the RV. Some of the kids are playing arcade games. Others are watching TV. One teacher flips burgers on the outdoor grill.

The RV goes flying backward into outer space. Then Uncle Grandpa slams on the brakes and the RV spins around. He stomps on the gas pedal again and they rocket away from the rumbling space station.

Pizza Steve hops up on the dashboard. "Sweet J-turn, Uncle G!"

That's when the space station explodes in a spicy flash of light and color. Big chunks of space station smack the rear of the RV, sending it careening off into space.

"Whee!" Uncle Grandpa cheers, thrilled by the impromptu twisty fun-park ride.

Kids go flying all over the living room of the RV.

A runaway burger hits Mr. Gus in the face.

When the RV straightens out, some of the kids are clutching their heads because they are dizzy. Others are clutching their stomachs because they are nauseated. Uncle Grandpa is neither of these things.

"Hey, kids!" Uncle Grandpa blurts happily. "We are LOOOOOST INNNNNN SPAAAAAAAACE! There's no way to get home."

"Oh no!" Sally wails.

"Don't worry," Uncle Grandpa soothes, appearing suddenly behind her head. He breaks off one of her pigtails and eats it. "Pizza Steve will find a way back to Earth."

"That's right, kiddos!" Pizza Steve calls from the front seat of the RV. "I'm the best RV space driver this side of the Milky Way. Hang on to your pepperoni!"

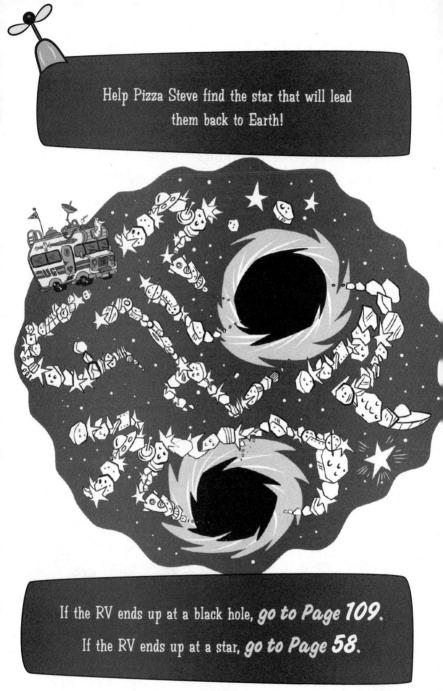

Help Pizza Steve find the star that will lead them back to Earth!

If the RV ends up at a black hole, *go to Page 109*.
If the RV ends up at a star, *go to Page 58*.

"Aha!" Uncle Grandpa cheers. "I've got it now." With a toothy grin, he turns to face the alien ambassadors and recites the alien text. *"Snorkle sneek. Skooble sneep sloop."*

The alien spaceships all stop fighting at once. Blobby ambassadors from both sides teleport into the RV.

"The one who is grandfather and also uncle has correctly spoken the ancient words." The red alien ambassador bows solemnly, as well as a giant blob creature can bow, anyway. "It is our sworn duty to end our conflict."

"Hooray!" Astro-girl Sally cheers. "Now these aliens can take us home."

The red alien ambassador continues. "Unfortunately, we do not know how to navigate you back to Earth."

"Oh no!" the rest of the kid astronauts wail. "Now what do we do?"

"Don't worry!" Uncle Grandpa gives them a reassuring smile. "I have an excellent plan."

⊘ ＊ COLLECT 12 BURRITO BADGES ＊ ○

Turn to Page 82.

"*Fighting is bad.* The aliens shouldn't fight!" Uncle Grandpa points a finger in the air. "I know how to handle this one."

Uncle Grandpa takes a megaphone out of the RV's glove compartment and smashes it through the windshield. The megaphone and Uncle Grandpa's hand grow until they are two times the size of the whole RV, then Uncle Grandpa stretches his lips until they're big enough to talk into the massive megaphone.

"Attention, aliens!" Uncle Grandpa booms in a commanding voice. "Stop this fighting at once. You all gotta get along."

The alien spaceships freeze in midair. The laser beams halt, as well. The red and blue aliens all turn to face the sound of the megaphone.

"Uncle Grandpa?" they ask in surprise.

"That's right!" Uncle Grandpa says.

One of the red aliens radios into the RV. "You can't make us stop fighting; you didn't say the magic words."

"Yeah!" a blue alien says, also radioing in. "The words are in our ancient alien scrolls."

A Space Helicycle zooms past the RV and tosses a scroll through the broken windshield. Uncle Grandpa and the rest of the gang examine the scroll.

"Ancient alien languages?" Pizza Steve laments. "So not cool."

"Uncle Grandpa . . ." Mr. Gus points at the weird black glyphs on the scroll. "You have to read these magic words, but we don't know how to read alien."

"That's okay," Uncle Grandpa says. "I have my universal translation dictionary right here." He rummages around inside Belly Bag and pulls out an enormous book. "This book can translate a million weird alien languages, like Orionese, Draconian, and French. Now let's see . . ."

The others hold their breath as Uncle Grandpa studies the alien scroll and the translation dictionary.

Match the alien glyphs and their English letters to decipher the alien words on the next page.

If you guess the translation wrong, *go to Page 116*.

If you guess the translation right, *go to Page 31*.

If something weird happens, *go to Page 46*.

Mr. Gus reaches out a hand and catches one of the falling stones. Then another. Then one falls from a section of the ceiling he hadn't expected it to, and it crashes to the floor.

"Oh no!" Mr. Gus roars in despair as the stones topple from everywhere, smashing through the floor of the cave. The whole gang tumbles through the air as the stones rain down around them.

When the dust settles, everyone groans to let the others know they're still alive.

Pizza Steve sits up. One of the lenses of his sunglasses has popped out. "Whoa. Tubular tumble."

Uncle Grandpa inspects their new surroundings. It's another cavern like the one above, but here there are even more crystals growing on the ground.

Mr. Gus bares his claws and tries to climb up the wall, but the stone is too hard and he can't get a good grip. "This is bad. We're trapped down here."

"Trapped?" Belly Bag laments. "Are we going to starve?"

"Don't worry, Belly Bag." Uncle Grandpa breaks off a chunk of one of the crystals and takes a big bite out of it. "We can eat this rock candy."

Mr. Gus stomps over to Uncle Grandpa. "Uncle Grandpa, I told you I don't think that's—"

Before Mr. Gus can say another word, Uncle Grandpa jams a handful of crystal into his mouth. It tastes so good, Mr. Gus nearly swallows Uncle Grandpa's arm. "Wow! This actually tastes really good."

"Let me have some!" Pizza Steve climbs on top of one of the crystals and starts eating his way down.

Giant Realistic Flying Tiger curls up by a few of the crystals and licks them with her kitty tongue.

Hours pass, then days. Uncle Grandpa and the others don't stop to sleep or bathe, they just keep eating the delicious crystals. Each one tastes better than the one before. Soon, they've eaten so many crystals that they are the size of beanbag chairs, lying on the ground, reaching to grab the next crystal.

Pizza Steve pats his oversize pizza belly. "Oh man. I couldn't crawl out of this cave even if I wanted to."

"I guess we're stuck here forever," Mr. Gus replies.

"No worries!" Uncle Grandpa says. "We can still eat more crystals."

"Ooh yeah, crystals!" cheers Pizza Steve.

THE END

"Pizza Steve has the right idea," Uncle Grandpa says matter-of-factly. "We should go to Mars for help. But first, we have to set the RV to interplanetary-travel mode."

Ding! The little video screen on the wall flashes. Now it reads: UNCLE GRANDPA'S SPECIAL COUNTER FOR WHEN HE USES BIG WORDS: 6. And then the 6 ticks up to a 7.

"Goody!" Uncle Grandpa smiles. "Three more and I get a free ice-cream cone!"

Uncle Grandpa releases the emergency brake on the RV. He revs the engine. He throws the lever to switch the RV into interplanetary-travel mode. Of course, a different Uncle Grandpa does each of these things. They all salute the Uncle Grandpa still standing with Pizza Steve and the others. "Ready to go, Uncle Grandpa!" they say in unison.

"Thanks, guys!" Uncle Grandpa hops behind the wheel of the RV and flies to Mars.

COLLECT 23 BURRITO BADGES

Go to Page 75.

Mr. Gus moves as fast as he can. The floor turns to quicksand, but he pulls through. Then the floor turns to water, but he swims through. Then Mr. Gus stumbles into a dark tunnel. He feels his way along the walls with his hands.

When the dinosaur man emerges from the tunnel, he is standing in a dark forest filled with tall trees. An owl hoots. Shadows dance in the moonlight. He realizes he has gone the wrong way.

"I need to get back to Uncle Grandpa," Mr. Gus says to no one in particular. He turns to face the tunnel once more, but the exit has disappeared. Uh-oh. Mr. Gus looks around, but he has no idea where to go.

"Screeeee!" a voice shrieks from above. Perched on a tree branch overhead is an enormous gray owl. It gnashes its narrow beak and glares at Mr. Gus with its wide, round eyes.

"What a hoot!" the owl says. "A tasty little dinosaur man lost in these woods."

"Ar-ar-are you part of Uncle Grandpa's virtual reality simulator?" Mr. Gus asks as he nearly shakes out of his dinosaur skin.

"SCREEEEE! Virtual? Maybe. Let's see what happens when I *virtually* eat you!"

"Gah!" Mr. Gus runs through the forest as fast as he can. The gray owl flaps its wings and gives chase.

Use this maze to help Mr. Gus find his way back to Uncle Grandpa.

If you end on an owl, *go to Page 48*.

If you end on Uncle Grandpa, *go to Page 13*.

"We have to get after that Earth! The world hangs in the balance . . . literally! We're the only ones who can save it . . . literally! I'm kind of hungry . . . literally!" He takes a bite out of a half-eaten pickle sandwich sitting on the dashboard. "Now, come on!"

The gang grabs hold of whatever they can find so they won't fall over. Uncle Grandpa throws the RV in reverse and slams on the gas pedal. They blast out of the space station and head back to Earth.

COLLECT 11 BURRITO BADGES

Go to Page 51.

Go to Page 51.

The Martian surface is quiet. The powdery red dirt is still on the windless terrain. Pizza Steve, Mr. Gus, and Giant Realistic Flying Tiger stand around, not knowing what to do next. Uncle Grandpa picks his nose.

"I kinda like it here," he says cheerfully. "Maybe we should move in."

"GrrrrrrrRROWL!" roars Giant Realistic Flying Tiger. She looks up at the sky, then back at Uncle Grandpa and the others, then the sky again.

"What's the matter?" Uncle Grandpa pulls a magnifying glass the size of a football stadium out of Belly Bag, holds it up to his face, and tilts it toward the sky.

Through the lens, Uncle Grandpa sees the Earth spinning dangerously close to the sun. He tosses away the magnifying glass. It smashes against the ground, causing a big earthquake, but no one pays attention to it. "Oh no! I forgot about the Earth. We're safe here, but Earth is in danger!"

Uncle Grandpa grabs his head and shakes it, while the others watch with concerned looks. All the thoughts in Uncle Grandpa's brain feel scrambled, and he can't make up his mind.

Unscramble the words in Uncle Grandpa's head to form a message, to help him make the right decision.

If you think the message says "WE ARE HOME,"
go to Page 92.

If you think the message says "HURRY HOME,"
go to Page 51.

Mr. Gus looks up into the eyes of the Martian princess. "I . . . Mr. Gus . . ."

Giant Realistic Flying Tiger glares at Uncle Grandpa.

". . . promise to uphold the virtues of the planet Mars."

Uncle Grandpa shakes his head. "Sorry, Tiger. Not this time. Mars needs Mr. Gus now. And I need this marzipan." He picks up a tube of marzipan and squeezes the whole thing into his mouth.

Mr. Gus bows his head low, taking his oath very seriously. "I will be strong. I will be brave. And I will lead us to a better future."

The princess smiles. "Arise, then, my king, and claim your weapon."

Mr. Gus climbs to his feet and takes the large battle-ax from her hands. He turns to face the crowd and roars. "YES! I am King Mr. Gus! I will lead you to the greatest future!"

Everyone cheers, except Giant Realistic Flying Tiger, who slinks out of the throne room with her tail between her legs.

Raising the battle-ax high above him, King Mr. Gus says, "Now hark—my first royal decree. I order a squadron of Martian astronauts to embark on a perilous journey to save the Earth. Do whatever you must. Spare no expense. Stop Earth from crashing into the sun!"

"Yes, sire!" A group of Martian astronauts rise from their seats in the audience and race out of the room. They return a few minutes later, their uniforms covered in soot.

"Your mission has been accomplished, sire." The Martian astronauts bow low at Mr. Gus's feet. "Our spaceships are equipped with high-powered tractor beams. We were able to pull your home world onto a new trajectory. Earth is now in a safe orbit around the sun.

"Whoo-hoo!" Uncle Grandpa cheers. Even Pizza Steve is impressed. Everyone applauds.

Mr. Gus nods at this happy news and sets down the battle-ax. "That's great! Thank you! See you later!"

Pizza Steve and Uncle Grandpa follow. Giant Realistic Flying Tiger is waiting for them at the exit. They don't even look back as they leave the Martian royal palace.

"Wait! WAIT!" The Martian princess chases after them, catching up to Mr. Gus on the drawbridge. "You are our king! You've just been crowned, and now you're leaving?"

"Yup!" Mr. Gus says. "I miss my home."

The Martian princess turns desperately to Uncle Grandpa. "Does this make any sense to you, Uncle Grandpa?"

Uncle Grandpa thinks. "Hmm . . . yup! Perfect sense."

The RV comes flying out of the sky and crashes into the drawbridge. It's still smashed up from its last crash landing. Now it's even more smashed up.

"Good morning!" Uncle Grandpa says as he climbs

aboard. The others pile in behind him. The busted-up RV sputters before taking off and heading back to Earth.

In the front seat of the RV, Mr. Gus pokes his head in while Uncle Grandpa drives.

"Hey, Uncle Grandpa," Mr. Gus says, looking rather shy. "Thanks for understanding my feelings back there."

Uncle Grandpa hops out of the driver's seat and stands beside Mr. Gus. He puts an arm around his shoulder. "No problem, Mr. Gus."

"It was hard for me to leave, but I really did want to go home."

"Uh-huh," says Uncle Grandpa.

"I guess it's kind of weird that I wanted to come home with my friends instead of staying on Mars and being king, huh? Did that surprise you, Uncle Grandpa?"

Mr. Gus looks over, only to discover that Uncle Grandpa still has his arm around Mr. Gus's shoulders, but he has detached himself from his arm and is back driving the RV.

"No way, Mr. Gus. That didn't surprise me at all!"

COLLECT 64 BURRITO BADGES

THE END

"This word is pretty hard," Uncle Grandpa says, pointing at a string of strange characters. "I think I know how it's pronounced, though." He takes a deep breath and makes a high-pitched squealing sound: "EEEEEEEEEEE EEEEEEEEEEEEEEEEEEEEEEEE!!!!!!!!"

The Astro School kids cover their ears. Giant Realistic Flying Tiger winces. The sound is so powerful, it knocks Pizza Steve onto his crust.

Uncle Grandpa's squeal is so intense, it rips a gap in the space-time continuum. A giant orange space sea urchin with a spiny purple shell spills out of the gap and floats before the RV in outer space.

"Hello, children! Aliens! Uncle Grandpa and friends!" The space urchin communicates through a telepathic link, pumped directly into everyone's brains.

"Hey, Space Urchin," Uncle Grandpa says with a friendly wave.

"I have brought you all presents: new spacesuits for the kids, food for the aliens, a sweet interstellar surfboard for Pizza Steve, next month's issue of *Teen Kewl Magazine* for Giant Realistic Flying Tiger (it's from the future!), and an old sock for Uncle Grandpa! I didn't get Mr. Gus a present because I knew he would enjoy feeling bad about not getting any presents."

"Wow . . . ," Mr. Gus says in amazement, a single happy tear rolling down his scaly cheek. "You know me so well, Space Urchin."

With a big lick of its orange tongue, the space urchin sprinkles the presents into outer space like magic.

"Thank you, Space Urchin! Thank you, Uncle Grandpa!" The red and blue aliens devour their food hungrily. "Who can fight when someone is giving you presents?"

"It's true!" The space urchin gloms on to the RV. "Now who wants to play video games?"

COLLECT 30 BURRITO BADGES

THE END

Mr. Gus scrambles through the forest,
swerving behind trees and ducking low to keep away from the
talons of the vicious owl.

But the bird of prey is at home in these dark woods, and
quickly catches up with Mr. Gus.

"Oh no!" Mr. Gus cries out as his foot gets caught on an
exposed tree root. He tumbles onto a bed of dry pine needles.

"*Scree!*" says the owl as it tosses Mr. Gus into its gullet.

Inside the owl's stomach, Mr. Gus sees a blinding light.
Blues and whites sparkle before his eyes. He's not in a
stomach at all, but floating through cyberspace. He's still
inside Uncle Grandpa's virtual-reality simulation.

Mr. Gus feels his file being transferred. And then, he
rematerializes at a hamburger stand. On a beach! It's beautiful
inside this simulation. There's hot cocoa to sip and suntan
lotion for his scales. There's a library with lots of good books
to read, and no Pizza Steves in sight! Yes, this is the most
peaceful simulation Mr. Gus has ever experienced, and he's
happy to let his feet sink into the sand and enjoy a good long
vacation.

THE END

The forty-seven Uncle Grandpa arms swing wildly at the flying Ping-Pong ball. The oozes trip all over each other, smooshing into each other and forming bigger oozes as they try to keep up with Uncle Grandpa's incredible skill.

When the smoke clears, the oozes have melted into puddles on the floor. Uncle Grandpa is breathing heavily. The forty-seven arms and their paddles retreat into Belly Bag.

After the oozes reconstitute themselves, they squish over to Uncle Grandpa, bubbling exuberantly. "That was the most extreme Ping-Pong playing we've ever seen! You may be the greatest Ping-Pong player in the universe, Uncle Grandpa!"

Pizza Steve slides into the conversation. "Well that's only because you haven't seen *me* play Ping-Pong. Ya dig?"

The oozes ignore him. "Uncle Grandpa, as you have bested us, we bestow upon you full citizenship of Gloptopia. You are one of us now."

"Okay, that seems great," Uncle Grandpa says.

"And to show our appreciation for your exceptional display of skill, we award you the title of Gloptopia's Official Ping-Pong Master."

"Also great." Uncle Grandpa gives Mr. Gus a high five.

49

The ooze gurgles, "And you will remain here forever, as our permanent Ping-Pong opponent!"

While no one was paying attention, one of the other oozes had seeped over Uncle Grandpa's feet. Other oozes wrap around the ankles of the rest of the gang.

"Hey, let us go!" Uncle Grandpa demands.

But it's no use. The oozes are already lining up for their next game of Ping-Pong.

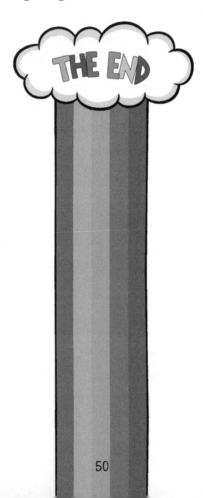

THE END

Back on Earth, the RV pulls up in front of the Poisson Yum, a world-renowned science think tank. It is part science lab, part astronomical observatory, and part fast-food fish restaurant.

Uncle Grandpa unbuckles his seatbelt and hops out of the RV. "These scientists and food entrepreneurs are the smartest people on the whole soon-to-be-destroyed-by-the-sun Earth! If anyone knows how to help us, it's them."

The gang walks across the freshly manicured lawn, which is turning from green to brown because the sun is getting closer and it's drying out the grass. Mr. Gus and Pizza Steve sweat profusely. It's getting hot.

The front door to the Poisson Yum flies off its hinges as Uncle Grandpa kicks it open. "Good morning!" he cheers.

Scientists run around in white lab coats, narrow black ties flapping over their shoulders. "No time to talk, Uncle Grandpa!" one of them says breathlessly as he runs by. "We're trying to save the Earth."

Uncle Grandpa and his friends wander around the lab, looking for some way to help. The lab is a total mess. Microscopes and test tubes and other science-y stuff cover the floor in a thick blanket of junk.

Two kid scientists approach Uncle Grandpa timidly. "Hey, Uncle Grandpa."

"Hey, Ted. Hey, Betsy. Aren't you a little young to have scientist jobs?"

"We're interns," Betsy explains. "You know, part-time, for school?"

"Oh right." Uncle Grandpa looks sheepish. "So how can I help?"

Ted tugs at his collar, hot in the lab coat with the sun so close. "Well, our boss told us to clean and sort all the loose equipment in the lab. There's a lot of clutter. But it doesn't seem important when there's so much danger from the sun."

"Don't worry, I will help you clean this clutter!" Uncle Grandpa puffs out his chest, ready to work.

"The kids are right, Uncle Grandpa." Mr. Gus peers out a window to see how close the sun is. "We have more important things to deal with right now."

Uncle Grandpa shouts so loudly his face turns red, and then his head morphs into a spicy chili pepper. "I SAID I'M GOING TO HELP CLEAN!" He starts scooping up all the clutter on the floor.

"No, Uncle Grandpa. Not that stuff." Betsy opens a closet door and a tidal wave of junk pours out, covering the floor. "This stuff!"

Uncle Grandpa's jaw drops as he looks at everything he has to clean. "Wow . . . it would take a tiny miracle to clean all that stuff up."

"*Did somebody say Tiny Miracle?*" The metallic voice belongs to none other than Tiny Miracle, everyone's favorite robot boy! Tiny Miracle sticks his round silver head through the window and then crawls inside with his long twisty legs. He plays catch with his head for a bit, tossing it from hand to hand and dribbling it like a basketball.

Uncle Grandpa scoots over to the robot. "Hey, Tiny Miracle. Can you help us clean up this mess?"

"*This looks like a job for Tiny Miracle!*"

Help Uncle Grandpa and Tiny Miracle clean up the lab. Do a word search to find all the science items that are scattered around. Words can be across, down, or diagonal.

If you find seven words or more, *go to Page 70*.

If you find fewer than seven words, *go to Page 11*.

Something is strange. On the other side of Giant Realistic Flying Tiger's wormhole is an Earth unlike the Earth of a few seconds ago. Everything is pink. The buildings, the oceans, and everyone's clothes—pink, pink, pink.

On every street corner, a different boy band is giving a free concert. They all look so dreamy!

Tiger purrs merrily as she walks down the street with Uncle Grandpa and the others. A shop across the street catches her eye, and she leaps through the open front door. The others follow her into the beauty parlor.

Everyone gets pedicures!

THE END

"You are going to love our planet!" the blue aliens assure Uncle Grandpa and the crew as the RV comes in for a landing on the Blue Goo Alien home world.

"Yes, yes!" says another alien. "It's the most fun place in three galactic sectors."

Pizza Steve flashes a big grin. "Well that sounds *totally* awesome. After all this time lost in outer space, I could use some fun."

Uncle Grandpa says, "Yeah, me too! We're all gonna have tons of fun on this alien planet."

"Even me, Uncle Grandpa?" asks Belly Bag hopefully.

"Even you, Belly Bag," says Uncle Grandpa.

When they land on the planet, the aliens give them all a grand tour.

One of the aliens points with a protrusion of goo at a massive wall. "Over there is one of our favorite spectator sports."

"X-treme rock climbing?" asks Pizza Steve.

"No, no. That's where we paint walls, and then watch the exhilarating race to see whose paint will dry first."

"You watch paint dry . . . for fun?" asks Mr. Gus.

"Sounds cool!" says Uncle Grandpa, not making any sense, as usual.

"And over here, we have our professional Knitting Stadium."

One of the other blue aliens leans close to Uncle Grandpa. "I've been trying to get tickets for months, but it's sold out."

"Now," says the lead alien. "After your boring adventure, I don't want to overstimulate you. Let's stand perfectly still for a while, and pass some time." The aliens all stand perfectly still, so that not even a ripple of their goo flesh moves. Uncle Grandpa and the others try to emulate their hosts.

"Huh-huh." Uncle Grandpa chuckles. "I'm a statue."

"This is so *boring*!" Pizza Steve complains.

Giant Realistic Flying Tiger roars in agreement.

"At least we're safe from the Earth crashing into the sun," Mr. Gus says.

But that doesn't stop Uncle Grandpa and the rest of the gang from being totally and completely bored for the rest of their lives.

THE END

The RV screeches to a stop in front of a bright white star. But there are huge spaceships on either side of the RV, and they are firing laser beams at each other. Pizza Steve has driven the RV right into the middle of an epic space battle!

Uncle Grandpa, Mr. Gus, and the Astro School students and teachers all pile into the front of the RV to watch the battle. The aliens look like giant, gooey pudding cups. Half of the aliens are bright red; the others are the color of blue jeans. The red aliens are flying spaceships that each look like a cross between a motorcycle and a helicopter.

"Sweet!" Pizza Steve gives himself a high five. "Those are *totally* rad space helicycles."

Meanwhile, the blue aliens are fighting in enormous mecha (giant fighting robots) that look like the members of the boy band One Direction. One of the robots snatches a space helicycle out of the sky and smashes it in its mechanical fingers. A squadron of space helicycles fires its lasers and vaporizes one of the singing robo-teenagers.

Pizza Steve says, "Those red aliens have the coolest spaceships ever. You have to help them, Uncle Grandpa!"

"Hmm . . ." Uncle Grandpa nods his head. Another Uncle Grandpa head pops out of the collar of his shirt and turns to Giant Realistic Flying Tiger. "What do you think, Giant Realistic Flying Tiger?"

The tiger roars her wise opinion.

"Well, obviously you think we should help the blue aliens win!" Pizza Steve raises his sunglasses to ensure that everyone can see him roll his eyes. "You love all that mushy boy band stuff that the blue aliens like."

Another head pops out of the second head's mouth, and stretches on a long shoelace of a neck to face Mr. Gus. "What do you think, Mr. Gus?" the third head asks. "What do you want to do?"

"I want to go home," Mr. Gus grumbles despondently.

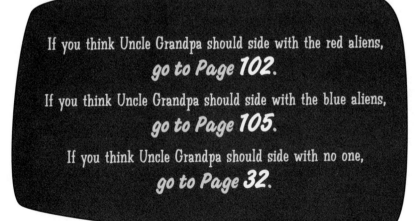

If you think Uncle Grandpa should side with the red aliens,
go to Page 102.

If you think Uncle Grandpa should side with the blue aliens,
go to Page 105.

If you think Uncle Grandpa should side with no one,
go to Page 32.

When Uncle Grandpa spent a semester at alien-language-translation college, he received perfect grades. So when he speaks to the ooze aliens in their native Gloppese, it's like everyone is speaking normally.

"Hey, ooze people! You can't keep us prisoner. I know your customs. First you must defeat us in the ultimate test of strength, speed, and skill. I, Uncle Grandpa, will be our champion, and I will face all of you in the most dangerous game."

Belly Bag quivers around Uncle Grandpa's middle. "But, Uncle Grandpa! The most dangerous game sounds, well . . . dangerous!"

"Don't worry, Belly Bag," Uncle Grandpa says soothingly. "You're going to help me win."

"ME?!"

One of the ooze aliens creeps forward to speak. Uncle Grandpa translates his words in his head. "You challenge us to a deadly competition of Ping-Pong?"

"Ping-Pong?" Mr. Gus, Pizza Steve, and Belly Bag ask in disbelief.

"Yep!" Uncle Grandpa says with a smile.

"You challenge *all* of us?" asks the surprised ooze.

"Yep!" Uncle Grandpa raises his hands, snapping the rope tying up the gang. An enormous Ping-Pong table materializes and falls from the sky, landing between Uncle Grandpa and the oozes. Small protrusions on each of the oozes extend and harden, forming slime-colored paddles. How is Uncle Grandpa going to play against all of them?

The answer immediately becomes clear when Belly Bag opens his mouth wide and forty-seven Uncle Grandpa arms reach out of him, each holding a stop-sign-red Ping-Pong paddle.

"Zero serving zero!" Uncle Grandpa declares as he slaps the small white ball across the table at his opponents.

Connect all the Ping-Pong balls using four straight lines without lifting your pencil from the page.

If you succeed, *go to Page 49.*
If you fail, *go to Page 67.*

The Martian warriors carry the gang

for several miles, down the other side of the mountain.
Giant Realistic Flying Tiger does not like being carried
by her four paws one bit, but Uncle Grandpa seems to be
finding the trip pleasant, so she keeps her fur smooth and
her head cool.

In the distance rises the Martian royal palace, a crystal
castle where the royal family of Mars lives. It is said that
the royal palace has some of the most beautiful rooms and
decadent feasts in the whole galaxy.

But the only room Uncle Grandpa and his friends
expect to see is the dungeon.

The bowels of the royal palace are dank and spooky. The
Martian jailers are hulking aliens in leather caps. They wear
weathered chain mail as armor. They carry whips and big
rings of iron keys on their belts. The warriors throw Uncle
Grandpa and his friends unceremoniously in a cell and
depart.

"Un-Un-Uncle Grandpa?" asks a timid and familiar
voice from one corner of the cell.

Uncle Grandpa squints into the darkness. "Who's
there?"

A boy steps into the torchlight. "It's me, Uncle Grandpa.
Benny. You know, Benny with the *awesome belly*?"

Benny pats his stomach happily. His belly is truly awesome, like a beach ball covered in skin.

"Benny!" Uncle Grandpa and Benny give each other a belly bump, happy to be reunited at last. A belly bump is like a fist bump, when you turn your belly into a giant fist and bump fist-bellies with a friend.

"How did you get stuck down here?" asks Mr. Gus.

"Oh, it was terrible!" Benny explains. "I was on Earth just minding my own business. I was pogo bellying. You know, when you bounce up and down on your belly like it's a pogo stick. Have you ever tried pogo bellying, Uncle Grandpa?"

"Nope! Can't say that I have." Uncle Grandpa quickly hides behind Mr. Gus a pile of trophies that say UNCLE GRANDPA FIRST PLACE POGO BELLYING CHAMPION.

"Anyway, I pogo bellied so high it shot me into outer space and I flew to Mars. The Martians found me trespassing and locked me up. It wasn't my fault! I didn't want to come to Mars. My belly just brought me here. You gotta help me, Uncle Grandpa. You gotta get me out of this dungeon."

"Consider it *done-geon*!" Uncle Grandpa says with a grin.

In the corner of the cell there's a small sewer drain covered in a metal grate. Uncle Grandpa walks over to it and inspects the drain. He thinks it probably leads into the main water system for the castle, and through a series of pipes, out of the castle.

"An escape route!" Pizza Steve gives a big thumbs-up. "I knew we'd find an exit."

Uncle Grandpa says, "Hey, Belly Bag, gimme that jar of sewer-grate remover."

"Sure thing, Uncle Grandpa! *Bleeeggggh!*" Belly Bag spits out a yellow jar, covered in slobber. Uncle Grandpa picks it up and twists off the lid. He reaches inside and pulls out a screwdriver.

Working quickly, Uncle Grandpa unscrews the sewer grate and tosses it aside. The gang peers into the drain.

"Nice thinking, Uncle Grandpa!" Benny squeezes between Mr. Gus and Giant Realistic Flying Tiger. "But how are we going to fit down there? I don't think there's any way we can fit down that hole, especially me with this big belly."

"No problem! Hey, Belly Bag, gimme that jar of fish sauce, will you?"

"You got it!" Belly Bag spits out a green screwdriver. Uncle Grandpa picks up the screwdriver and breaks it in half. Fish sauce oozes out of the broken tool.

"Fish sauce?" Mr. Gus asks, puzzled.

"Huh-huh! Yup!" Uncle Grandpa splashes them all with the gross-smelling fish sauce. Instantly, they all transform into fish. Dinosaur fish, pizza fish, tiger fish, boy fish, and Uncle Grandpa fish. They start hopping down the drain one by one, escaping their cell.

A big smile passes over the fat-lipped face of the Uncle Grandpa fish. "Last one in's a rotten egg . . . oh!" He looks around and realizes he's the only one still in the cell. He briefly morphs into a big green egg radiating with stink, but then turns back into a fish and jumps in after his friends.

Help Uncle Grandpa and his friends find their way through the drainpipes and out of the castle on the next page.

If you end up at Exit A, **go to Page 104**.
If you end up at Exit B, **go to Page 94**.
If you end up at Exit C, **go to Page 86**.

Uncle Grandpa plays Ping-Pong like he is part ninja, part robot, and all energy drink. His forty-seven hands move like leaves in a tornado, spinning about, slapping the ball back at the oozes.

But the oozes consider Ping-Pong the official pastime of their species. They work together to return each volley from Uncle Grandpa.

Soon, dozens of balls are flying through the air, then hundreds. Uncle Grandpa tries to return each ball, but his forty-seven hands aren't fast enough. Every white ball hits Uncle Grandpa in the face. They stick in his skin, which mushes like mud, collecting all the balls in a big pile before Uncle Grandpa topples over and lands on his back, arms splayed out.

Uncle Grandpa strains and all the balls pop out of his face, returning it to its original handsome shape. "Wow, that was a fun game!"

Belly Bag pulls all the Ping-Pong-playing Uncle Grandpa arms back into his frowning mouth. "But Uncle Grandpa, you were supposed to win!"

"Oh yeah, I forgot. Oh well!"

Mr. Gus and Pizza Steve grimace, knowing they may be in for a terrible fate.

The oozes huddle around Uncle Grandpa. One of them speaks. "Dear Mister Uncle Grandpa. We have bested you."

"Yeah, I know," Uncle Grandpa says.

"But we appreciate you giving it the old Uncle Grandpa try. As a result, we will show you to the exit, as a token of our appreciation for giving us such non-oozy competition."

"YAY!" cheers the whole Uncle Grandpa gang.

The oozes lead Uncle Grandpa and the others to the exit of the vast and intricate cave system. Finally, at the end of a long tunnel, they see an opening that leads back to the Martian surface.

"Hey look, it's Mars again!" Uncle Grandpa points at the exit. "Follow me! Thanks, oozy Glop people."

The gang scrambles up the tunnel and bursts onto the rocky terrain of the Martian surface. They stand around, catching their breath and looking at each other. They made it through the cave. At last!

⊘ * COLLECT 15 BURRITO BADGES * ●

Go to Page 41.

Pizza Steve adjusts his cool shades and struts toward the Martian warriors. "'Sup, guys? It's me, Pizza Steve! You know, the *coolest* guy on Mars?"

The lead warrior pounds the dirt with the butts of his spears. "We know nothing of this 'Piece of Steve.' Why do you trespass on the sacred mountain of Mars?"

Mr. Gus grumbles to himself. This is what he was afraid of. Uncle Grandpa watches the scene with wide, dopey eyes. "I think it's going really well!"

Pizza Steve tries to explain the situation. "You see, our home planet is totally off course and about to be cooked by the sun. We came to you cool aliens for help. You're not as cool as Pizza Steve, but you're still pretty cool."

"We are very cool!" the Martian warrior growls. "And you are still trespassing. Take them to the dungeon!"

"Hey, man," Pizza Steve backs away. "Not cool."

With four arms each, it's very easy for the aliens to grab the gang by their hands and feet and carry them away.

⊘ ✳ COLLECT 2 BURRITO BADGES ✳ ○

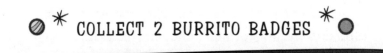

Go to Page 62.

"And that's the last one." Uncle Grandpa has a satisfied smile on his face as he puts away the final microscope. Tiny Miracle is wriggling around the room and doing a little dance. They finished cleaning up the science lab in record time!

Betsy and Ted run over to Uncle Grandpa carrying a book, *Wormhole Navigational Research*. "Hey, Uncle Grandpa! Look what we found while we were cleaning."

"You found it!" exclaims one of the older scientists, who has just walked into the room. "We've been looking for that book for years. Bring it here. It might contain what we need to save the Earth."

More scientists pile into the room and crowd around the book. They say very intelligent things like "My word!" and "Oh yes, I see."

The group forms a circle so the scientists can explain what's going on. Uncle Grandpa takes off his head and puts it in the middle of the circle so he can see everyone and follow along.

An older scientist says, "Our only chance to save the Earth is to create a wormhole and send the Earth through it before we all get swallowed by the sun. The formula to create a wormhole is very complicated, but it is in this book. We have to work together to crack it."

The scientists give Uncle Grandpa and his friends a page of the book to crack the formula.

Cross out all the Uncle Grandpas to spell out the answer to the code.

A R U N T C G H E
O C N Y A W L C U
L A C A B T L H
O W I C O N T S

If you think it says "Run the calculations,"
go to Page 22.

If you think it says "Trust Uncle Grandpa,"
go to Page 78.

Uncle Grandpa isn't quite sure about some of the foods on the table, but that's okay! He throws a bunch of his favorites onto the plate for the coronation. Jelly and ketchup and turkeybread all pile on, along with marshmallow ferrets and tomato leather shaped like a roll of paper towels.

All the foods start getting mashed together as Uncle Grandpa piles more and more on top. Soon the pile grows so big, it forms a gigantic food monster.

"*Bleeyaaagh!*" screeches the food monster as it smashes the table in two. It climbs off the plate, growing so large it fills the whole kitchen.

"Uh-oh!" cheeps Uncle Grandpa.

From far away, Martians see the giant food monster burst through the roof of the castle, sending turrets flying like pieces of a broken toy. The food monster was sick of always being eaten. But now he was big, and hungry, and he was going to have his revenge.

Tasty, tasty revenge.

THE END

Pizza Steve turns to talk to the Martian warriors, but Uncle Grandpa is already sitting in a circle with them. They're playing an elaborate version of "patty-cake." Uncle Grandpa has sprouted two extra arms so he can play along.

"Yay!" Uncle Grandpa cheers. "I love patty-cake!"

"We love you, Uncle Grandpa!" the Martian warriors say.

Pizza Steve awkwardly tries to squeeze into the circle. "Hey, guys. Whatcha playing? Patty-cake? That's totally cool. Almost as cool as *Pizza Steve!*"

"Never heard of him." The lead Martian warrior doesn't even look up from his game of "patty-patty-cake-cake" with Uncle Grandpa.

"But it's me!" The talking foodstuff's voice quivers. "I'm Pizza Steve."

"You're not even a monkey's uncle," another Martian warrior says. "Or a space monkey's uncle, or whatever."

Mr. Gus scratches his gut. "Hey, Pizza Steve, I thought everyone on Mars knew you."

Pizza Steve shrugs off his encounter with the aliens. "Yeah! Can't you tell? They're playing a supercool game with me, because they know they're not cool enough to act like they know someone as cool as me."

Uncle Grandpa appears between them. His four hands

are bright red from the rough clapping with the Martian warriors. "Hey, guys. These warriors are going to take us to see the Martian princess."

"The princess!" Pizza Steve sweats profusely. "I'm sure she'll remember me! Heh-heh."

COLLECT 15 BURRITO BADGES

Go to Page 8.

The dusty surface of Mars is quiet and peaceful, with big rock formations every few miles. Suddenly, the sound of a sputtering RV with rocket engines breaks the silence.

Uncle Grandpa's RV falls like a comet, slamming into the ground and making a huge crater. When the dust settles, the RV is all smashed up. The doors have fallen off. Uncle Grandpa opens a door that isn't there and steps onto the surface.

Pizza Steve does a triple front midair somersault and lands in a karate pose. "That's one small step for me, one giant leap for pizza-kind."

Giant Realistic Flying Tiger floats in front of them. If it weren't for her rainbow trail, it would be hard to see her because her orange stripes blend in really well

75

with the surface of the planet. She roars so loudly the sound echoes off the rocks.

"Tiger's right." Uncle Grandpa nods vigorously. "We need to look for help so we can stop the Earth from crashing into the sun."

"We *have* to go over there, Uncle Grandpa." Pizza Steve points at a dark cave in the distance. "All the *coolest* Martians hang out in caves."

Mr. Gus points in the other direction. "There's a big mountain over that way, Uncle Grandpa. If we climb it, we can get a view of the whole area."

"Hmm . . ." Uncle Grandpa ponders his options. "These are both pretty good ideas. What do you think, Uncle Grandpa?"

The Uncle Grandpa standing next to Uncle Grandpa says, "I think the cave, obviously."

"He means the mountain," says a third Uncle Grandpa, on the other side of Uncle Grandpa. "Look, I've got my hiking boots and everything."

Uncle Grandpa sighs. "Oh, Uncle Grandpa, you're no help at all."

Which Uncle Grandpa should Uncle Grandpa trust?

If you think the gang should go to the cave, *go to Page 98.*

If you think the gang should climb the mountain, *go to Page 110.*

Uncle Grandpa looks up from his page of the book, feeling positively enlightened. The others hold their breath as they wait for him to speak.

"I figured it out!" he says. "We don't need to calculate anything at all. I can open a wormhole whenever I want."

"Really? That's *totally cool*," says Pizza Steve.

But before he can finish saying that, Uncle Grandpa is already dangling from the ceiling fan. "Yep. I do it all the time."

"Well, there's no time to lose, Uncle Grandpa." Mr. Gus waves for Uncle Grandpa to come down from the ceiling fan. He drops to the floor with a crash.

"But there's one last important question," Uncle Grandpa says. "Where should the wormhole go? Hmmm?"

They all think about their absolute favorite places, and what their ideal world would be like if they could create one from scratch.

"Okay," Uncle Grandpa says, clenching his fists. "Now I'm going to think real hard and create a wormhole to a place that has everything you're all dreaming of.

POP! POP-POP!

When Uncle Grandpa opens his eyes, he realizes he made a mistake. There isn't one wormhole, but three. Each one looks like a whirlpool floating in the middle of the room. One of them is floating in front of Giant Realistic Flying Tiger. Another is just over Pizza Steve's head. The third is just behind Uncle Grandpa's butt.

Uncle Grandpa scratches his giant chin. "Hmm . . . looks like I couldn't get them all together. Oh well! I guess we'll just have to choose one, and that's the wormhole I'll send the Earth through."

If you think Uncle Grandpa should choose Giant Realistic Flying Tiger's wormhole, *go to Page 55*.

If you think Uncle Grandpa should choose Pizza Steve's wormhole, *go to Page 115*.

If you think Uncle Grandpa should choose his own wormhole, *go to Page 12*.

Uncle Grandpa pushes open the door

to the kitchens in the Martian royal palace. The Martian princess stands with Mr. Gus and Pizza Steve, going over the menu for Mr. Gus's coronation as the king of Mars.

"You see," the princess explains, "during the coronation everyone celebrates by throwing food at the king—it's quite delicious. But we have to sort out foods His Soon-To-Be Highness won't like."

Mr. Gus studies the assortment of food on the table. "I can't say I've ever been a fan of fruits."

The Martian princess combs through her hair with her fingers, suddenly becoming aware of the number of bananas and berries on the table. "Fruits? But they're so sweet! It is very difficult to grow fruits on Mars. Still, I will respect your wishes, Mr. Gus. I will separate the fruits for you."

"Good morning!" Uncle Grandpa says, plodding toward the group. "I can help! I'll get rid of all these fruits."

"Oh, that is very kind, Uncle Grandpa." The princess links her arm with Mr. Gus. Pizza Steve looks on sadly. "We will be in the throne room. Guests are already arriving for the coronation. Do not delay."

"I'll be done in a jiffy!" Uncle Grandpa assures her. As they depart, Uncle Grandpa studies the table of food.

This shouldn't be too hard. But he can't mess up! Everyone is counting on him. He has to finish and hurry to the coronation.

Separate the food so that fruits go to the trash and non-fruits go onto a plate.

If six or fewer fruits end up in the trash,
go to Page 72.

If seven or more fruits end up in the trash,
go to Page 18.

Uncle Grandpa, Mr. Gus, Pizza Steve, Giant Realistic Flying Tiger, Belly Bag, and all the kids from Astro School work together to build a restaurant in this distant corner of the cosmos. Without a way home, stuck out in space, they might as well try to make a few space bucks, right?

They name the restaurant Uncle Grandpa's Arm Pitstop. Uncle Grandpa grows to the size of a gas-giant planet like Jupiter, orbiting an enormous star. They build a gas station in the wedge of Uncle Grandpa's armpit, and then the restaurant inside the gas station. It all makes total sense, of course.

Inside the restaurant, a smaller Uncle Grandpa and the gang grill up tasty canned chicken nuggets and the house specialty—chipotle mayonnaise on a stick.

On the day the restaurant opens, the Astro School kids are happily flipping nuggets in the back, while Uncle Grandpa welcomes the first customers inside. Both the red aliens and blue aliens have sent delegations, complete with their own popular food bloggers.

"Very tasty nuggets!" the red alien food critic says. "Just like my mother used to can. I give this new establishment four stars!"

The blue alien food critic wipes his mouth with a napkin, and the crumpled paper gets stuck in his slimy cheek, but he doesn't seem to mind. "These mayo sticks are succulent! Four stars!"

"Wow, Uncle Grandpa!" Mr. Gus's eyes go wide in amazement. "You finally found something the blue and the red aliens could agree on."

"Yup!" Uncle Grandpa cheerfully pops a nugget into his mouth. "It was all part of my delicious plan!"

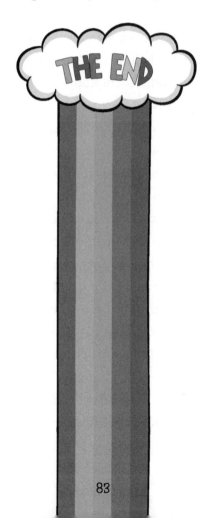

THE END

"Games it is, then!" Uncle Grandpa opens his mouth to say "YAY!" but when he does, his tongue rolls out and a little Uncle Grandpa is standing on it. The little Uncle Grandpa flaps his little arms and says, "Yay!" in a little, squeaky voice.

The crowd of students and teachers follows Uncle Grandpa through the halls of the Astro School space station. Mr. Gus, Pizza Steve, and Giant Realistic Flying Tiger take up the rear, not sure what to expect.

Uncle Grandpa leads the group inside the Challenge Room, a huge virtual-reality simulator that's kind of like a school gymnasium but also an arcade and filled with fun (but challenging) things to do.

With a snap of Uncle Grandpa's fingers, the plain gray walls of the Challenge Room jump to life. Thousands of dazzling colors light up the sky around the group. Metal platforms whiz overhead. Rings of fire spin in the air. Mr. Gus squints at all the digital fireworks and electric mayhem. It's hard to believe all of these effects are created virtually by a computer.

"Whoa! WHOA!" The Astro School student Sally starts to float in the air. "Check it out. I can fly!"

Sally clenches her fists and two jets of fire burst out the bottom of her space boots. She darts around the room like a dragonfly.

"Check this out!" One of Sally's classmates, Bartleby, makes a fist and it grows until it's the size of a car. He swings his giant hand and punches a tower of tacos piled nearby. The delicious tacos crunch and go flying into the walls.

Mr. Gus looks around in surprise. It appears everyone has developed some sort of superpower. The speedy students race. The strong ones wrestle. The other flying students chase Sally through fiery rings that float in the air. Uncle Grandpa dances, quite pleased with everyone playing his games.

Even Pizza Steve has gained a power. He stretches out his pizza body until he's the size of a castle wall. "Hey, Mr. Gus. Check me out! I'm *Deep Dish Steve!*"

Mr. Gus runs in terror as one of Pizza Steve's doughy feet crashes to the ground.

✳ COLLECT 15 BURRITO BADGES ✳

Go to Page 38.

Go to Page 38.

"Whee!" The Uncle Grandpa fish goes flying out the bottom of the long drainpipe, bouncing off the rocks outside the Martian royal palace.

The fish all land in a pile. Flopping about on dry land has never been less fun.

With one of his fins, the Uncle Grandpa fish reaches inside the Barnacle Bag on his belly and pulls out a can of Not Fish Anymore Sauce.

After sprinkling it all over himself and the other fish, they quickly turn back into their normal selves, except they all still have a big craving to eat worms.

"Good morning!" the not-fish-anymore Uncle Grandpa says cheerfully.

"Oh, thank goodness. You're the best, Uncle Grandpa!" Benny pounds the ground with his big belly triumphantly. "I'm free! Hooray!"

"That's right! But now it's time to go home." Uncle Grandpa reaches into Belly Bag and pulls out a rocket ship that's shaped like a fish with an enormous belly.

"Thanks, Uncle Grandpa!" Benny waves good-bye

before his rocket blasts him off into space, far away from Mars.

Uncle Grandpa smiles as he watches him go. Another kid has been saved!

 COLLECT 15 BURRITO BADGES

Go to Page 41.

"Stop that coronation!" Uncle Grandpa rises from his seat and points a finger at the Martian princess.

Dozens of Uncle Grandpas—dressed in fancy suits and armor and dresses—turn, shocked at the interruption, and *shh* Uncle Grandpa.

"I will not *shh*!" Uncle Grandpa says. "Mr. Gus, do not say those words. Do not touch that ax. You Martians keep all crowns away from my friend!"

Giant Realistic Flying Tiger purrs. Uncle Grandpa glances at her and winks.

The princess shouts, "Guards! Seize that Uncle Grandpa! Silence him at once!"

Laser beams shoot through the air as the Martian warriors open fire on Uncle Grandpa. He hops on the back of Giant Realistic Flying Tiger, who zooms around the room trailing rainbows, knocking over the Martian warriors with her tiger-y girth.

"Yay!" the crowd of Uncle Grandpas cheers, having totally forgotten how mad they were at Uncle Grandpa a moment ago.

"All right!" Pizza Steve pumps his fist as the action unfolds. "Totally sweet escape plan, Uncle Grandpa!"

They fly over Pizza Steve and grab him. Then they fly over Mr. Gus. Uncle Grandpa picks him up by the tail and swings him onto Giant Realistic Flying Tiger's back. The Martian princess shrieks and swings her ceremonial battle-ax angrily at them.

Tiger bursts through the ceiling and flies far away from the Martian palace.

The gang races across the Martian landscape, finally landing on the peak of Olympus Mons, the tallest mountain in the solar system. Night falls, and they set up camp.

As the twin moons of Mars drift lazily across the sky, Uncle Grandpa roasts a cup of hot dogs over the fire. He's happy that the gang is all still together. Giant Realistic Flying Tiger is happy that the Martian princess is gone. Pizza Steve is happy that if he didn't become the Martian king, no one else did, either.

Mr. Gus is not happy. He's definitely *un*happy. But Mr. Gus is always unhappy, so it's really no big deal.

Everything is fine! The cup of hot dogs tastes great. Nothing could possibly go wrong.

Back on Earth, everyone whips out their suntan lotion as their planet goes flying into the fiery yellow star.

With Uncle Grandpa's advice fresh in her mind, Sally flies in her spaceship back to the big fleet of other Astro School spaceships where all her classmates are waiting.

"Hey, everyone!" Sally calls over the radio. "We gotta hop up and down on the Earth. Come on!"

The ships fly to the South Pole, which has become the South Puddle. The sun is so hot and close that the waters are nearly boiling. Every glacier on the planet has melted.

All the Astro School spaceships point nose down at Earth and begin slamming into the surface as hard as they can. Like a thousand silver pogo sticks, they bounce off Earth faster and more forcefully. Soon they are all moving in unison. They knock Earth into a new orbit.

But as it curves around the sun, Earth gets dangerously close to those harsh solar rays. The trees burst into flames. The dirt turns black and charred. The seas evaporate, leaving behind a lot of salt and very startled fish. The squids really don't like it.

Later, the whole group is standing on top of a burnt mountain, watching a blazing hot sunset. Uncle Grandpa is still playing his pocket video game.

Mr. Gus rubs his belly in discomfort. "Uncle

Grandpa! Look what happened. The whole Earth . . . it looks barbecued."

"Yeah," Uncle Grandpa says lazily. "Deep-fried Earth tastes better, but I guess barbecued will do. Anyone got any hot sauce?"

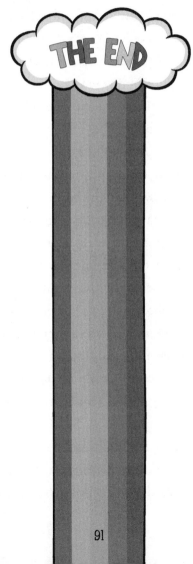

THE END

Uncle Grandpa looks up from his intense concentration. He has a twinkle in his eyes and a smile on his face. "I've got it! I know what we're going to do."

Pizza Steve steps closer. "What's that, Uncle G?"

Kneeling down in front of his friend, Uncle Grandpa says, "Pizza Steve, good buddy, you and me are gonna build a zero-gravity fun park. A fantastic place where humans can chill after Earth goes boom!"

"Totally *rad*!" Pizza Steve cheers.

When Pizza Steve looks up, two hundred Uncle Grandpas stand in rows at attention. Each Uncle Grandpa wears a yellow hard hat and carries a big wrench, a hammer, or a screwdriver. "Let's get to work!" they all shout in unison.

Like a vast colony of ants in rainbow suspenders, the Uncle Grandpas scurry across the Martian surface, constructing the elaborate fun park. They build roller coasters without any rails. There's a Ferris wheel that spins in midair, totally disconnected from the ground. In the zero-gravity obstacle course, bouncy islands float among even bouncier platforms. The Uncle Grandpas hop from island to island, laughing.

At the grand opening, all the different Martian aliens come to play. The park fills up fast. Pizza Steve rakes in a bazillion Martian bucks in admission fees. It seems like a pretty happy ending for everyone.

On a rocky outcropping overlooking the fun park, Mr. Gus gazes at the small pale sun in the sky. A heavy frown never leaves his face. The fun park is cool and all, but he misses the Earth.

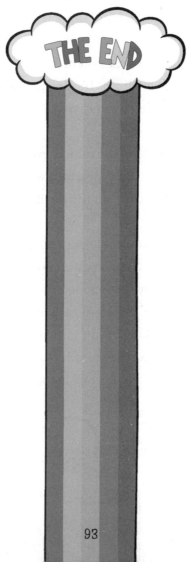

THE END

After several hours in the tunnel, the Mr.
Gus fish gets the sense that something is wrong.

"Uh, hey, Uncle Grandpa? I think we may have been
down this pipe before."

The royal palace's sewer system is a maze of connecting
pipes. It's easy to go in circles. It's obvious now that they've
been looping through the same stretch of tunnel for a long
time.

After several weeks in the tunnel, everyone gets wise
that there's a problem. They look for a way to get out of the
loop of pipe, but they can't find any exits no matter how
hard they try.

After several months in the tunnel, they are all pretty
tired, and they've pretty much given up on ever getting
out of the tunnel. They find enough stuff in the pipes to
eat, so it's no problem, as long as they remain fish forever.
Surely the Earth has long been cooked by the sun, but they
wouldn't know, because they're still stuck.

The loop just keeps going and going and going and . . .

THE END

Inside the space station, kids rush through the metal hallways. They hurry to fit their bulbous helmets over their heads. The air is rapidly leaking out of the big hole the RV punched into the station.

The hood of the RV sticks through the hole. The front of the vehicle opens like a big mouth. Uncle Grandpa steps out and into the space station, followed by Mr. Gus, Pizza Steve, and Giant Realistic Flying Tiger.

One of the girls stops short when she sees them. She takes off her oddly shaped space helmet, which has special spaces for her blond pigtails.

"Uh, Uncle Grandpa?" the girl asks quizzically.

"Hey, Sally," Uncle Grandpa says with a toothy grin. "Looks like there's a hole in your space station."

"Well of course there is!" Sally screeches. "You put it there with your big, stupid RV!"

"What is this place, anyway?" Mr. Gus asks, looking around at all the kids in spacesuits and the large posters featuring pictures of cats and encouraging words about self-esteem.

Sally pulls on her pigtails in frustration. "It's Astro School, you green goof! Haven't you ever heard of Astro School? It's where the smartest kids on Earth go to receive astronaut training."

"Smartest *and* coolest," Pizza Steve adds. "Yep. I went to Astro School when I was just a ball of dough."

Giant Realistic Flying Tiger growls skeptically.

A teacher stops short when she sees them all standing there. She has a big beehive of pink hair. "Uncle Grandpa! You have to help us evacuate the space station." She waves for all of the kid astronauts to crowd around. "Quick, children, climb aboard Uncle Grandpa's RV. We have to get out of here. The leaks are going to cause the station to run out of air."

"Oh." Uncle Grandpa frowns. "I kind of like the space station with no air. Then we can do this." He holds his breath and his face shrivels up, turning purple as a prune.

"That is hardly something for the children to do!" the teacher says in a huff.

"Hey, Uncle Grandpa." Mr. Gus points toward the big hole the RV has made, and then at all the broken pieces of metal on the ground. "You could use this broken wall to patch up the space station. Then we wouldn't have to evacuate."

"Hmm . . . that's a pretty good idea, Mr. Gus. Let me think."

"Hurry, Uncle Grandpa!" Sally and the other astronaut kids wail.

"Okay, okay, sheesh!" Uncle Grandpa says.

See the hole in the wall of the space station and the broken pieces on the floor. The pieces fit together like puzzle pieces. If the pieces all fit, choose to stay. If the pieces don't all fit, don't stay.

If you think Uncle Grandpa should evacuate the space station, *go to Page 28*.

If you think Uncle Grandpa should stay on the space station and try to fix it, *go to Page 14*.

Uncle Grandpa leads the gang across the Martian wastes to the cave. Stalactites hang down from the cave entrance like the fangs of a vampiric fish.

"This way, everyone," Uncle Grandpa urges. He pulls on his ear and his eyes illuminate, becoming the headlights of a car.

"Yeah!" Pizza Steve saunters into the cave like he owns the place. "I'm a *champion spelunker*. This is going to be so cool."

"Just stay together," Mr. Gus says. "We don't want to get lost down here."

Underground, the cave is quiet. Uncle Grandpa lights the way. They pass by a garden of strange crystals that shine pretty colors when the light hits them.

Uncle Grandpa snakes his tongue out of his mouth and licks one of the crystals. "Mmm! Rock candy."

Mr. Gus makes a face. "Actually, Uncle Grandpa, I think that's just a rock."

In the next room of the cave, the ceiling is paneled with dark stones. Suddenly, a loud rumbling noise fills the cave. The ceiling starts to collapse! The dark stones fall, smashing into the ground.

"Look out, Uncle Grandpa!" Mr. Gus raises his muscular dinosaur arms and holds the stones in place so they won't fall. But there are too many! Mr. Gus realizes that he only needs to hold the stones that are falling. But he has to hurry!

The stones on the ceiling are falling, but only the ones with an odd number of sides. Can you help Mr. Gus figure out which stones he has to hold up?

If you think Mr. Gus needs to hold up five stones,
go to Page 35.

If you think Mr. Gus needs to hold up six stones,
go to Page 26.

"Please, Uncle Grandpa!" the Astro School kids beg and whine. "Please, oh, please, you have to help us save the Earth."

Uncle Grandpa scratches his forehead. "Yeah, okay."

With that, Uncle Grandpa leaps through the gummed-up wall, breaking it apart into chunks of metal again. He hops into the RV and races after the Earth. Mr. Gus, Pizza Steve, Giant Realistic Flying Tiger, and the kids and teachers from Astro School all follow in spaceships from the Astro School Docking Bay.

Pizza Steve spirals through space in his ship, which looks like a flying saucer painted to resemble a pepperoni. "Hey, check it out! I'm a space pizza. This flying saucer is *totally cool.*"

"Careful, Pizza Steve," Mr. Gus grumbles over the spaceship radio.

"Wha—" Before Pizza Steve can react, he crashes into an asteroid and goes spinning off into space.

"Hey, it's cool!" Pizza Steve says over the radio. "I did that *so* on purpose."

The rest of the spaceships follow Uncle Grandpa back to Earth.

Mr. Gus and Sally pull up in their spaceships next to the RV. In the driver's seat, Uncle Grandpa is playing on a pocket video game machine. Uncle Grandpa is really good at this video game, because he is using ten thumbs to mash the buttons all at once.

"Uncle Grandpa!" Sally shouts belligerently over the radio. "What do we do? How do we save the Earth from crashing into the sun?" She looks worriedly at the sun, which is taking up most of the sky now because Earth is getting so close.

"Jump up and down on it," Uncle Grandpa mutters without looking up from his game. On the screen, a tiny pixelated Uncle Grandpa is jumping up and down on a turtle shell.

Sally's eyes go wide. "Jump up and down on it. Of course!"

"Uh, Sally, wait!" From his spaceship, Mr. Gus tries to get Sally's attention. But it's too late.

⊘ ✳ COLLECT 31 BURRITO BADGES ✳ ⬤

Go to Page 90.

"Those red aliens need our help to defeat those giant robot monsters!" Uncle Grandpa shouts. "But fortunately, we have giant robot monsters of our own."

The roof of the RV flips up like a catapult. Dozens of insectoid robots fly through space, latching onto the blue aliens' giant robots. The robot bugs chew through the robot pop stars as easily as termites chew through wood.

"Bleep blorp!" the blue aliens wail over their digital communicators. "Fall back! Retreat! Run! Split! Get out of here! Go! Depart! Evacuate! Escape! Flee!"

"Hey, nice robots!" Pizza Steve grins.

"Hey, nice thesaurus," Uncle Grandpa says.

Uncle Grandpa's robot bugs return to the RV, but once everything is back to normal (assuming "normal" means having an RV floating through outer space) and the blue aliens are gone, there's a knock on the outside of the RV.

Dong! Dong!

The living room windows slide open and the red aliens ooze inside. There's not much room for them, so the astronaut kids scrunch against the walls to make space.

"Greetings, humanoids, dinosaurs, tiger, pizza slice, and Uncle Grandpa. You defeated our foes, and so we are in the debt of you." The middle of the lead alien's three eyes swells to the size of a watermelon when he speaks. "We had been battling the blue aliens for three-point-squid eons. At last, you have put an end to the conflict."

Mr. Gus scratches his chest. "What were you all fighting about for that long?"

The red alien licks its ruby lips. "We red aliens are always hungry. The blue aliens taste delicious. The blue aliens never expressed a desire to be eaten by us, but one day we made a monumental discovery: We did not *need* the blue aliens' permission to eat them. And so we fought, but still we never had the chance to eat the blue aliens. And now, thanks to you, we never will."

"Gee, that's too bad." Uncle Grandpa grins. "Guess you'll be hungry now."

"Contrarily!" the red alien says. "We may not have any blue aliens to eat, but a piece of pizza, a tiger, a bunch of Earthlings, a dinosaur, and an Uncle Grandpa will suffice sufficiently."

Swelling up very large, the red alien turns to his companions. "Sound the dinner bell, boys! It's gobbling time!"

THE END

The Uncle Grandpa fish squints in the dark drainpipe.

"I think the exit is this way!" he says as bubbles come out of his fish mouth.

The Mr. Gus fish, Pizza Steve fish, Giant Realistic Flying Tiger fish, and Benny fish follow the Uncle Grandpa fish. The Uncle Grandpa fish picks up speed and crashes through the grate at the bottom of the pipe.

In the brightly lit room that lies beyond, the fish fly through the hole and land on smooth white tiles. They flop around on the floor to the Martian shower room helplessly.

Soaped-up Martians scream and run away in fright. "Quick!" one of them shouts. "Get the sewer-fish catcher!"

The Uncle Grandpa fish's gills flare nervously. Uh-oh! Looks like they made a wrong turn somewhere.

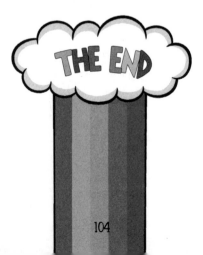

As Uncle Grandpa watches the battle unfold, the red alien space helicycles pummel the blue alien space robots. Uncle Grandpa feels a pang of sympathy for the on-the-ropes blue aliens.

"We must help the blue aliens!" he shouts.

Giant Realistic Flying Tiger purrs appreciatively.

"Throw the lever!" Uncle Grandpa bellows.

"Which lever?" shouts little astronaut Sally.

"All the levers!" Uncle Grandpa answers.

The kids open all the closet doors, revealing large walls covered in brightly painted iron levers. They flip the down ones up and the up ones down.

Two long arms sprout out the sides of the RV, and two muscular mechanical legs pop out of the back. The front cab of the RV tilts downward, forming a head. In fewer than eight seconds, the RV morphs into a totally rad battle bot.

Uncle Grandpa twirls in a circle on one foot, points a finger in the air, and pokes himself in the nose, posing like a nautical lunar body. "Mega RV Zero, charge!"

The giant RV robot sticks out its tongue and keeps pulling on it, making it longer and longer. The RV starts spinning its tongue in a circle until it makes a huge fan that blows the red alien spaceships far away.

Amid the cheers of the Astro School students, a

holographic display screen lowers from the living room ceiling. A half dozen blue aliens squeeze together so they all appear on camera.

"Thank you, Uncle Grandpa!" the blue aliens say. "You've saved us. Please, you and your friends must come live with us on Blue Alien Planet, where you will be our honored guests."

"Nah, I'm good!" Uncle Grandpa says simply.

The blue aliens begin to cry gooey blue tears. "Waaaah! Oh, please, Uncle Grandpa? Please come with us!"

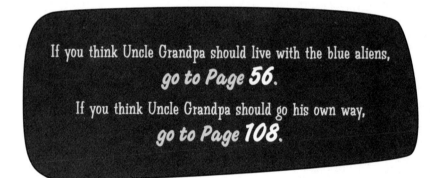

If you think Uncle Grandpa should live with the blue aliens, *go to Page 56*.

If you think Uncle Grandpa should go his own way, *go to Page 108*.

Uncle Grandpa speaks, but the oozes don't pay any attention to the words coming out of his mustached mouth. Giant Realistic Flying Tiger roars impatiently.

"I'm *trying*, Tiger!" Uncle Grandpa huffs. "I guess I mixed up my words the wrong way."

The oozes turn and glide across the stone floor to the stalagmite where the gang is imprisoned.

"Now and Grandpa Uncle," the lead ooze sputters. "Is it one time to become the with ooze."

The oozes surge over the gang like waves of thick snot, covering every inch of their bodies. The ooze soaks into Tiger's fur. It wraps around Mr. Gus's tail. It adds unspeakably gross toppings to Pizza Steve. Uncle Grandpa's mustache tingles as the ooze creeps over his face, into his mouth, and up his nose.

Mr. Gus roars, "Argh! Uncle Grandpa! They're absorbing us into the ooze."

"Yeah, but it kind of tastes good," Uncle Grandpa says around a mouthful of ooze. "Huh-huh! That tickles."

Uncle Grandpa and the gang melt away and become one with the ooze. But at least now they can understand what the oozes are saying!

"DELICIOUS!"

THE END

Uncle Grandpa grimaces, not wanting the smooshy-gooshy, ooey-gooey-bluey aliens to cry. "Sorry, alien people! We really can't move to your home planet."

The blue aliens emit a distressed gargle. Mr. Gus opens the door to the RV and lets them return to their space mecha.

"Glad that's over!" Uncle Grandpa says. "I really just want to go back to Earth."

The little astronaut girl Sally tugs on Uncle Grandpa's rainbow suspenders. "But, Uncle Grandpa! How are we going to get home? None of us know the way."

"Oh yeah, I forgot about that." Uncle Grandpa grins. "But don't worry! We can go on an intergalactic road trip!"

And so the RV begins the greatest road trip (in space) ever to enter the annals of cosmic history. Uncle Grandpa and his band of intrepid explorers race black holes, navigate quasars, and dance with supernovas! It is a very long journey—one perhaps too big for a single story—but it is an adventure that surely no one on the RV will ever forget.

The RV flies through space, nearly reaching the speed of light. The melted cheese starts oozing off Pizza Steve's body.

Then he sees it—up ahead is a giant black hole! The massive vortex of antimatter is sucking everything into it.

"Whoa! Totally the opposite of cool, right up here!" Pizza Steve flings the steering wheel all the way to one side, and the RV flips, tumbling end-over-end through space.

Back in the living room, the kids all go flying again. Two burgers hit Mr. Gus in the face. Uncle Grandpa sits calmly, picking pieces of burger off Mr. Gus's face and eating them.

The RV tumbles into the black hole. It spirals down the drain just like when Uncle Grandpa flushed his toy RV down the toilet.

THE END

The mountain is sloped, with rocky outcroppings across its surface, so the climb is not too difficult. Giant Realistic Flying Tiger can fly, anyway, so for her it's supereasy. She leads the way, scouting a path to the summit.

When they reach the top of the mountain, a group of Martian warriors is waiting for them. The green-skinned creatures are over eight feet tall and carry hunting spears in each of their four hands.

"Look! It's Uncle Grandpa!" One of the gruff aliens points with his spear.

"Hey, alien people. " Uncle Grandpa waves.

Pizza Steve slicks back his crust smoothly. "Relax, everyone. Don't forget, Pizza Steve is the coolest guy on Mars. I'll handle this *negotiation*."

Mr. Gus doesn't like this situation one bit. "I don't know. They already recognized Uncle Grandpa. Maybe he should be the one to talk to the aliens."

"I'm hurt, Mr. Gus!" Pizza Steve poses defiantly. "Diplomacy is my middle name."

If you think Pizza Steve should talk to the Martians, *go to Page 69*.

If you think Uncle Grandpa should talk to the Martians, *go to Page 73*.

Uncle Grandpa follows Giant Realistic Flying Tiger's rainbow trail through the castle, arriving at a napping room. Thick pillows are strewn about, and comfy blankets are available for use on the shelves that line one wall. Tiger is half-buried under a pile of pillows, her realistic tail poking out.

A big pillow flops down next to Giant Realistic Flying Tiger. She looks up and sees that the pillow is Uncle Grandpa. It has his eyes and mustache and his big mouth.

"Hey, Giant Realistic Flying Tiger! What's wrong?"

"Rowl!" she roars.

"You don't want Mr. Gus to become the king of Mars?"

"Roar!"

"Well why not?"

"GrrrrrrrRROWL! ROAR!"

"Hmm . . ." Uncle Grandpa thinks carefully. "That's a pretty good point."

Whenever Uncle Grandpa talks to Giant Realistic Flying Tiger, he always ends up contemplating the meaning of the universe and all existence. She's a very wise Giant Realistic Flying Tiger. This time, however, she makes Uncle Grandpa contemplate not just the universe, but the whole situation with Mr. Gus and the Martian princess.

"Gee, Tiger, maybe you're right." Uncle Grandpa's

head spins around three times, like he's a windup toy getting ready for a big move. "Okay! I promise to stop the coronation. There's no way I will let Mr. Gus become king of the Martians."

COLLECT 5 BURRITO BADGES

Go to Page 18.

When Uncle Grandpa opens his eyes,

he's in a big cavern dotted with sparkling pools of slime. Standing in the pools are the ooze aliens known as the Glops. They are bickering about something in their strange scrambled speech.

Uncle Grandpa tries to run away, only to discover he is tied to a big stalagmite with Mr. Gus, Pizza Steve, and Giant Realistic Flying Tiger.

"We gotta get outta here!" Uncle Grandpa says. "Hey, Glops! Let us go!"

Two of the aliens exchange an oozy glance. "Prisoner want what does? All speech mixed is his up."

Uncle Grandpa pokes Belly Bag. "Quick, Belly Bag. Get my Glopese-to-Uncle Grandpa translation dictionary."

"Sure thing, Uncle Grandpa." Belly Bag unzips his mouth and sticks out his tongue, revealing the leather-bound *Seventeenth Edition Gloppese-to-Uncle Grandpa Translation Tome*.

Uncle Grandpa flips through the pages frantically. "Let's see . . . there has to be some way to do this."

Help Uncle Grandpa unscramble the oozes' speech.
What are the oozes trying to say?

If the oozes are saying, "We want to eat you for dinner,"
go to Page 107.

If the oozes are saying, "We want to eat dinner with you,"
go to Page 60.

Uncle Grandpa pulls Earth through Pizza Steve's wormhole. When he opens his eyes, he watches his feet sink into the sidewalk. It's made of melted mozzarella. Cars whiz by on pepperoni wheels.

"Hey, look!" A pack of fifteen schoolgirls, all slices of pizza, run up to the group. "Look! It's Pizza Steve. Oh-Em-Gee, he is *so* cool."

"WAAAH! Take a selfie with me, Pizza Steve."

Snapping his fingers, Pizza Steve says, "Chill, ladies. There's plenty of Pizza Steve to go around."

While Uncle Grandpa lies on the ground and waves his arms, making cheese angels, and Pizza Steve runs off with his fans, Mr. Gus looks around. There's an outdoor cafe nearby with checkered tablecloths. Good, he thinks. He's superhungry.

But then he sees two pieces of pizza on a date. They're eating people!

Where did that wormhole take them?

Uncle Grandpa completes his translation and uses the megaphone to announce the magic words. "Borgle bloop!" he says. "Gurgle, blargle blook!"

Instantly, ambassadors of both the red and blue aliens teleport into the RV.

"Borgle bloop?" the blue alien ambassador asks. "Are you sure?"

"That's what I said." Uncle Grandpa nods. "I hope it brings peace to your people."

"It does! It does!" the red alien ambassador cheers. "Your statement has made us agree on something for the first time in many solar rotations."

"That peace is the answer?" Mr. Gus asks hopefully.

"No!" the red alien ambassador says. "Uncle Grandpa has volunteered you all as rations for our hungry astro-blob-people."

"Hooray!" the blue alien ambassador says. "Uncle Grandpa has ended the famine!"

"Oh no!" Mr. Gus says. "Uncle Grandpa, you must have gotten your translation of the alien scroll wrong."

But Uncle Grandpa isn't listening. He is splashing a whole bottle's worth of hot sauce onto his arm. "Oh well! I'm sure I'll taste great. Hey, aliens, is it okay if you make me a burrito?"

"Whatever you want, Uncle Grandpa," says the red alien ambassador with a hungry grin. "I'm sure you'll be delicious no matter what."

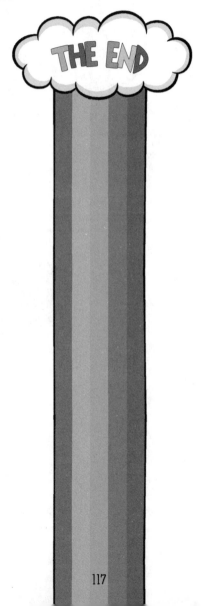

THE END

Oh boy, burritos!

How many burrito badges did you collect? Add up all the
ones you earned and figure out your burrito badge total.

So how did you do?

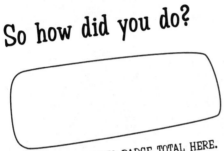

WRITE YOUR BURRITO BADGE TOTAL HERE.

Want to get more burrito badges?

Flip back to *page 1* and begin the adventure again,
making new choices.

Answers

page 25

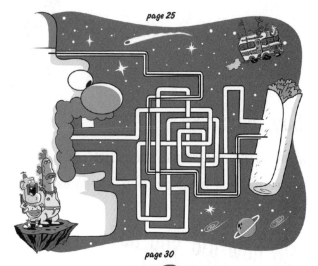

page 30

page 34

S N O R K L E   S N E E K

120

Answers

page 39

page 42

HURRY HOME

page 54

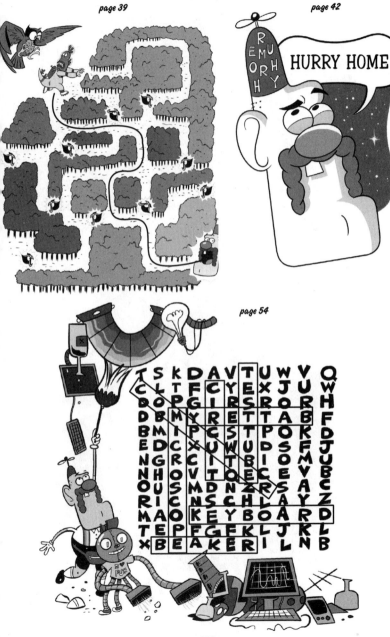

Answers

page 61

page 66

Answers

page 71

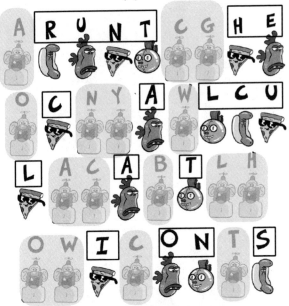

A R U N T C G H E
O C N Y A W L C U
L C A B T L H
O W I C O N T S

RUN THE CALCULATIONS

page 81

Answers